KIDS' SPORT STORIES

FOOTBALL DREAMS

Written by Shawn Pryor

illustrated by Genevieve Kote

raintree

a Capstone company — publishers for children

Raintree is an imprint of Capstone Global Library Limited, a company incorporated in England and Wales having its registered office at 264 Banbury Road, Oxford, OX2 7DY – Registered company number: 6695582

www.raintree.co.uk
myorders@raintree.co.uk

Designed by Ted Williams
Original illustrations © Capstone Global Library Limited 2020
Originated by Capstone Global Library Ltd
Printed and bound in India
982

978 1 4747 9375 9

British Library Cataloguing in Publication Data
A full catalogue record for this book is available from the British Library.

CONTENTS

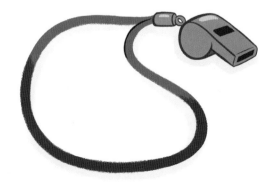

Glossary

 **goal** area within which players must put the ball to score

 **goalkeeper** player who protects the goal and tries to stop the other team scoring

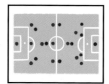 **position** part someone plays on a team; each position has a set job to do and needs different skills

 **save** move that stops the other team scoring

 **striker** player whose main job is to score; also called a forward

Chapter 1
MAKING A CHOICE

Keisha was at the Sports Fair with her parents. Children could sign up for a team sport. There were so many sports to choose from! Keisha wanted to find the right one for her.

Her mother pointed at one of the team tables. "Keisha, would you like to play hockey?" she asked.

"No," Keisha said. "That's not my thing."

Her father pointed at another table. "How about the swimming team?" he asked.

Keisha shook her head. "Swimming is fun, but water gets stuck in my ears," she said. "And that makes me grumpy."

"So, no swimming," said her father.

Golf was also a no. So were gymnastics
and tennis.

Suddenly, Keisha grabbed her mother's
hand and pulled. "Mum! Over here!
Hurry!" she said.

Keisha and her mum ran down a long
row of tables. Her dad followed.

"Slow down," Keisha's mum said. "If you want to sign up for athletics, you've just run passed that table!"

Keisha finally stopped. In front of her stood a boy bouncing a football on his foot. He did all sorts of tricks with the ball.

"I want to play football!"
Keisha shouted.

Keisha's parents looked at her and grinned. "Really?" they said together.

Keisha smiled. "I watch football with Grandad all the time," she said. "He played when he was at school. I want to be a striker and score goals like Grandad! Sign me up!"

Chapter 2

STRIKING OUT

Keisha and her teammates stood in
a circle. They bounced on their toes.
Football practice was so exciting! Every
day they learned something new.

"Today we'll see what position suits you each best," Coach said. "Every position on the pitch is important."

"I want to score goals!" Keisha said.

"Me too!" said Tyler.

Coach spun the football in her hands. "The first position we're going to try is the striker," she said. "Line up!"

Keisha raced to the front of the queue.

"Show us what you've got, Keisha!" Coach said.

Coach rolled the ball towards Keisha.

Keisha made an amazing kick. It hit the back of the net!

"Great goal!" Coach said.

The rest of the team took their turn kicking the ball. A few minutes later, Coach blew her whistle.

"Now let's look at your passing skills," she said. "Find a partner and start passing to each other."

Tyler and Keisha paired up. Tyler kicked the ball. Keisha caught it with her hands.

"You can't catch the ball. You have to stop it with your feet, chest or head," said Tyler.

Keisha's face felt hot. "Sorry," she said. She rolled the ball back.

"It's OK," Tyler said. "Let's try again."

Tyler kicked the ball to Keisha a second time. She caught it again.

"Sorry," Keisha said.

Coach blew her whistle. "Let's do some running!" she shouted. "Strikers need to be quick. Line up across the middle of the pitch!"

The children lined up. Keisha knew she had to win this race. She had to show Coach she would be a brilliant striker.

"When I blow my whistle, run to the goal line and back," said Coach.

WHOOOOOOSH!

The children sped off! Keisha kept up at first. Then she fell behind. Her teammates passed her.

Keisha finished second from last.

Chapter 3

KEISHA'S A KEEPER

After the race, Coach gave the news to the team. "Tyler, Anna and Seb, you will be our strikers," she said.

"Fantastic!" said Tyler.

"Amazing!" said Anna and Seb.

Keisha walked away with her head down.

"Let's take a short break, everyone," Coach said.

Coach walked over to Keisha. She asked what was wrong.

Keisha wiped away her tears. "I'm not a striker," she said. "I wanted to be like my grandad."

Coach put her hand on Keisha's shoulder. "Remember what I said earlier?" she asked.

Keisha nodded. "Every position is important," she said.

"That's right!" Coach said. "You've got some good skills, Keisha. You're strong and you can catch the ball really well."

"But we aren't allowed to catch the ball," Keisha said.

"Strikers aren't, but goalkeepers are," Coach said. "They stop the ball from going into the net. Come here. Let's try something."

Coach walked Keisha to the goal. The rest of the team watched.

"OK, Keisha," Coach said. "I'm going to kick the ball. You stop it."

Keisha's stomach twisted and turned. She didn't know if she could do it. Coach kicked. The ball flew towards the goal.

Keisha jumped, reached and made
a diving catch!

"I caught it!" she shouted.

"Nice hands, Keisha! Brilliant save!"
Tyler said.

One by one, Coach and Keisha's teammates tried to score a goal. Keisha blocked every shot.

"Keisha's amazing!" Seb said.

"With practice and help from your teammates, Keisha, you'll get even better," Coach said.

Keisha smiled. "Thanks, Coach," she said. "Being a goalkeeper is fantastic! I can't wait to tell my grandad. And I can't wait to play my first game!"

RED LIGHT, GREEN LIGHT

Dribbling is a basic football skill that helps you move the ball down the pitch in a controlled way. To dribble, use the inside or top of your foot and tap the ball. Use both feet and try not to look at them while dribbling. Keep the ball in your control.

Gather a few friends and give this game a try. You'll have fun and build skills, too!

What you need:
- a large grassy area
- a football for each person

What you do:
1. Line up your friends shoulder to shoulder. Each person should have a ball at his or her feet.
2. Walk 40 steps away and stop.
3. With your back to your friends, shout "Green light!" At this signal, everyone dribbles towards you.
4. After a couple of seconds, shout "Red light!" At this signal, everyone must stop.
5. When you have shouted, turn around quickly. See if you can catch someone who's still moving. Anyone caught moving must go back to the starting line.
6. Repeat steps 1 to 5 until someone reaches you. Then pick a new person to be "it".